Sneezy Louise

written by **Irene Breznak**

illustrated by **Janet Pedersen**

RANDOM HOUSE 🏠 NEW YORK

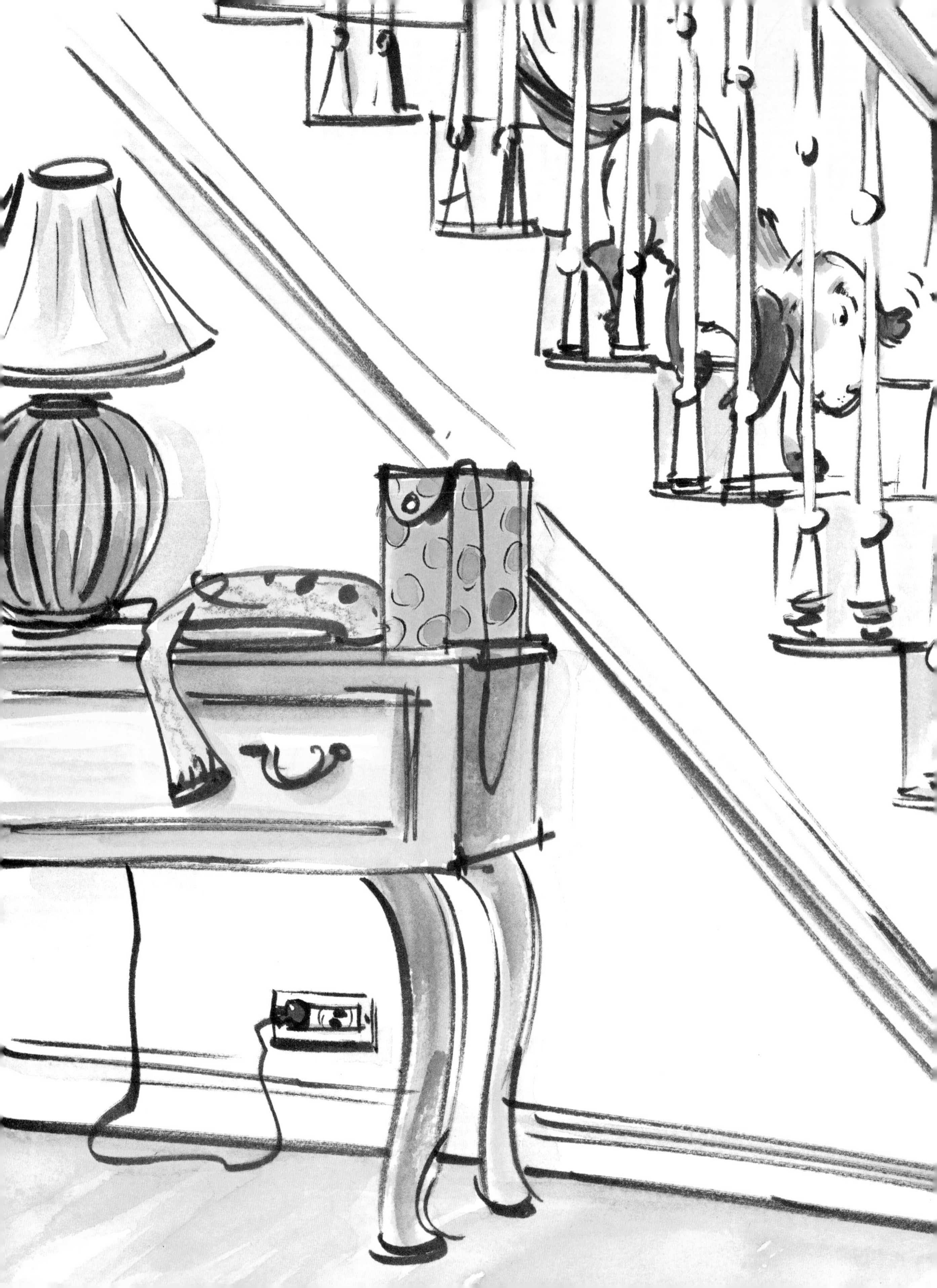

As Louise stumbled down the stairs for breakfast, she knew, *she just knew,* that this wasn't going to be an easy day. Her eyes were itchy, her throat was wheezy, and her nose was very, very sneezy.

Louise shuffled to the table in her purple flowered pj's. She knew, *she just knew,* that Mommy would give her oatmeal with raisins for breakfast instead of her favorite Coco Crunch cereal with pink marshmallow stars.

As Mommy placed the bowl of oatmeal in front of her, Louise's eyes got itchy, her throat got wheezy, and her nose got sneezy. She knew that she was going to . . .

Oatmeal splattered everywhere!

"Geez, Louise! **COVER YOUR MOUTH, PLEASE!**" Mommy said
in a not-so-good-morning voice.

Later that morning, Louise knew, *she just knew,* that it wasn't going to be an easy day at Wilson Elementary School. She lost her new glitter pencil somewhere in her messy desk, and she couldn't get her printing to fit between the lines. And she knew, *she just knew,* that Mrs. Graham would pick her best friend, Mary, to collect everyone's spelling lists instead of her.

As Mary carried the stack of papers past her desk, Louise's eyes got itchy, her throat got wheezy, and her nose got sneezy. She knew that she was going to . . .

Papers scattered everywhere!

"Geez, Louise! **COVER YOUR MOUTH, PLEASE!**" Mary bellowed in a not-so-best-friend voice.

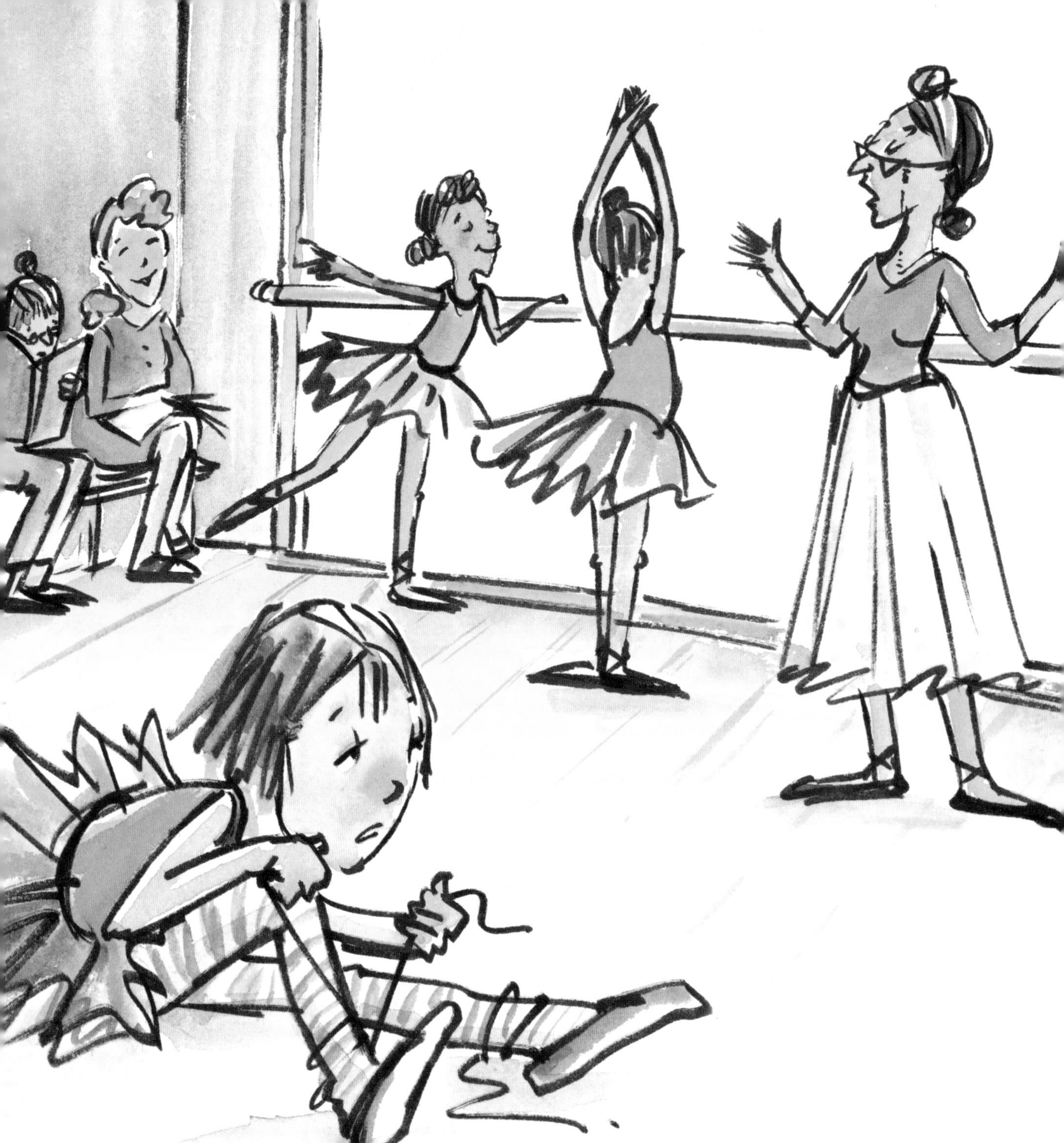

After school, Louise knew, *she just knew,* that it wasn't going to be an easy ballet practice. As Mommy proudly looked on, Louise knew that Madame Claire was going to make them practice pirouettes. Louise hated pirouettes.

When the other ballerinas scurried around to form the very straightest line, Louise's eyes got itchy, her throat got wheezy, and her nose got sneezy. She knew that she was going to . . .

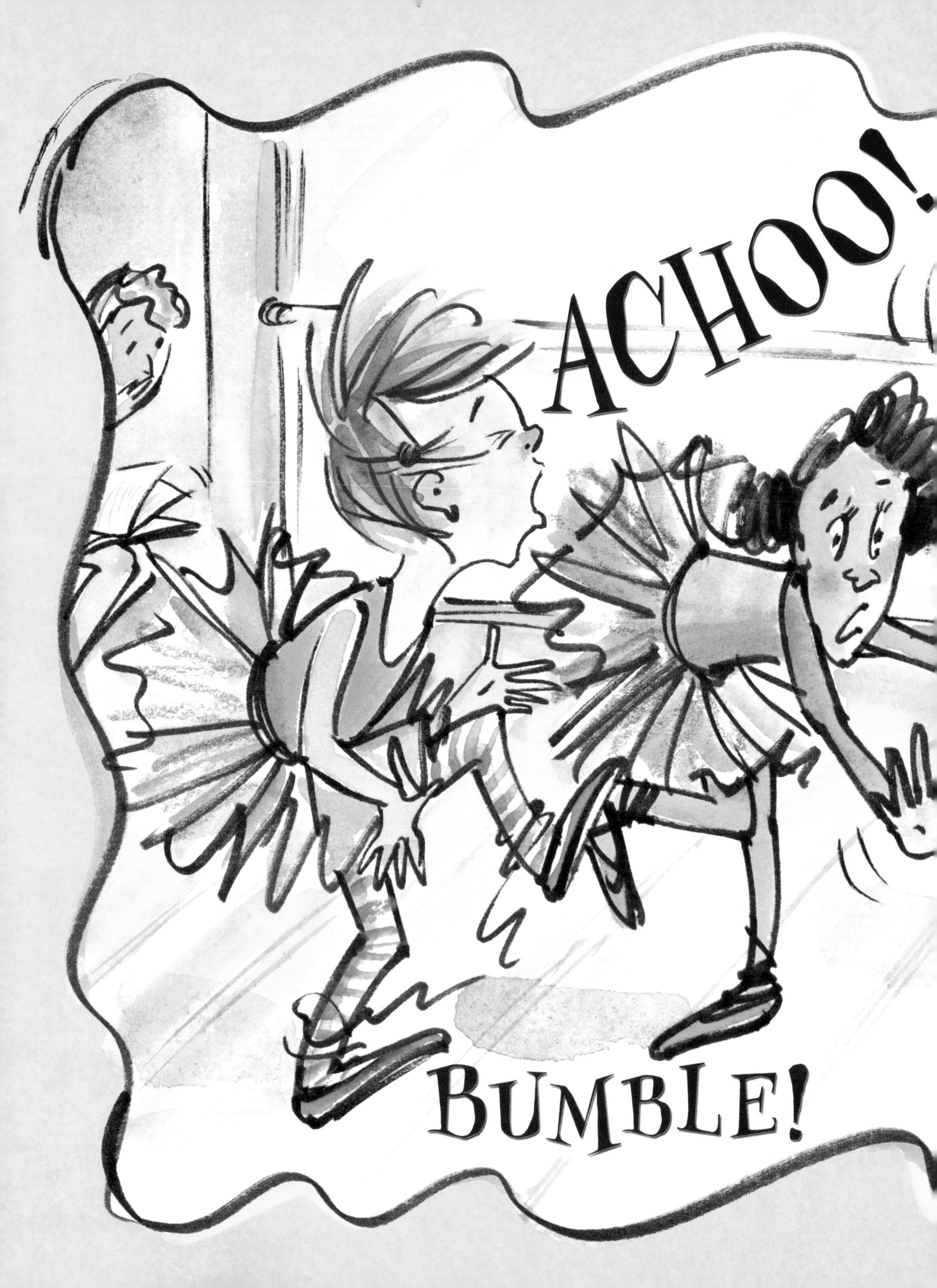
ACHOO!
BUMBLE!

Louise stumbled into Keisha, who pushed into Zoe, who tripped over Juanita, who landed right on top of Amanda!

"Geez, Louise! COVER YOUR MOUTH, PLEASE!" shouted Amanda in a not-so-ballerina voice.

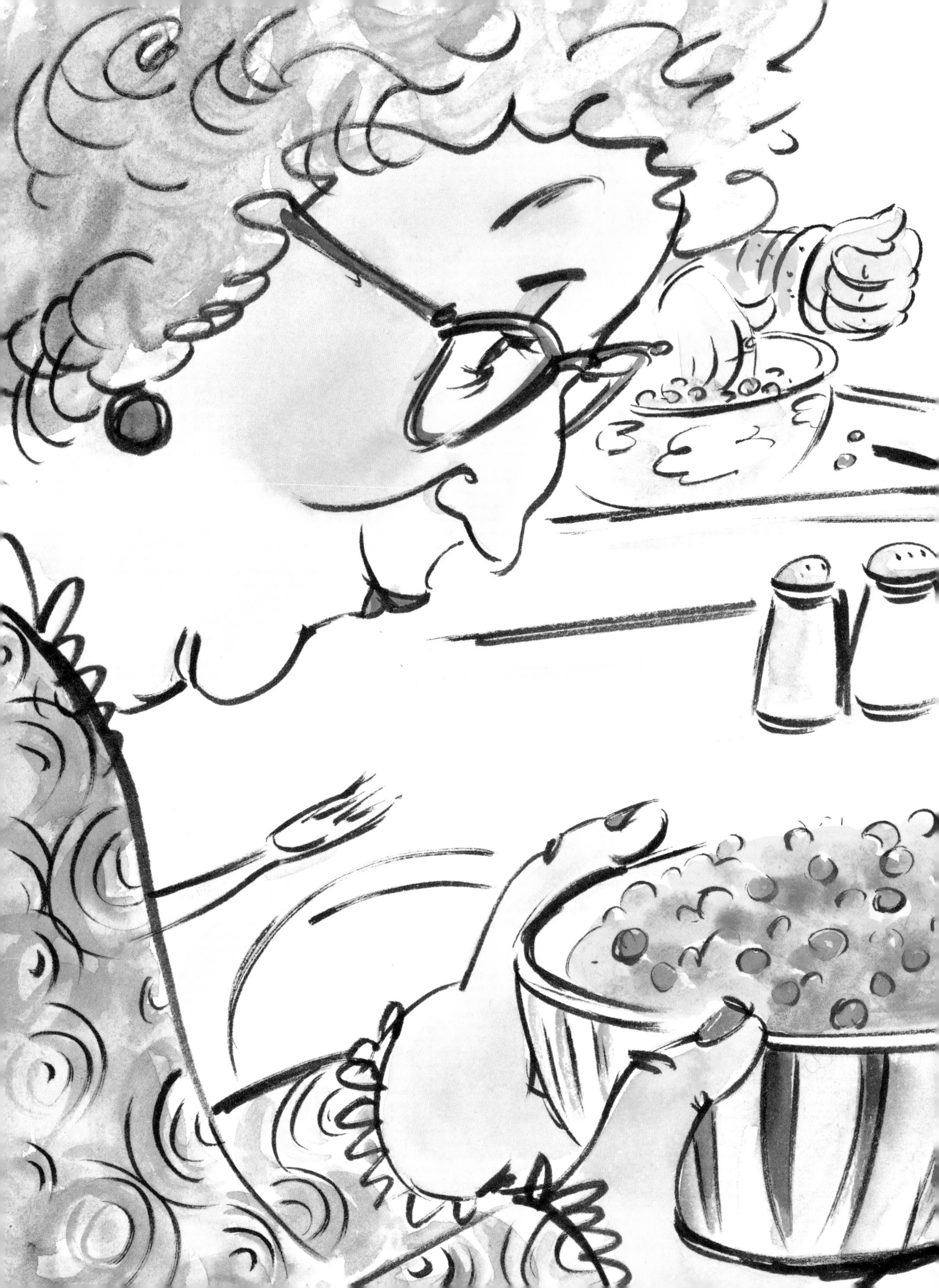

At the dinner table, Louise knew, *she just knew,* that it wasn't going to be an easy meal. As Grandma passed her the bowl of peas, Louise's eyes got itchy, her throat got wheezy, and her nose got sneezy. She knew that she was going to . . .

Peas bounced everywhere!

"Geez, Louise! **COVER YOUR MOUTH, PLEASE!**"
Grandma sternly whispered in a not-so-Grandma voice.

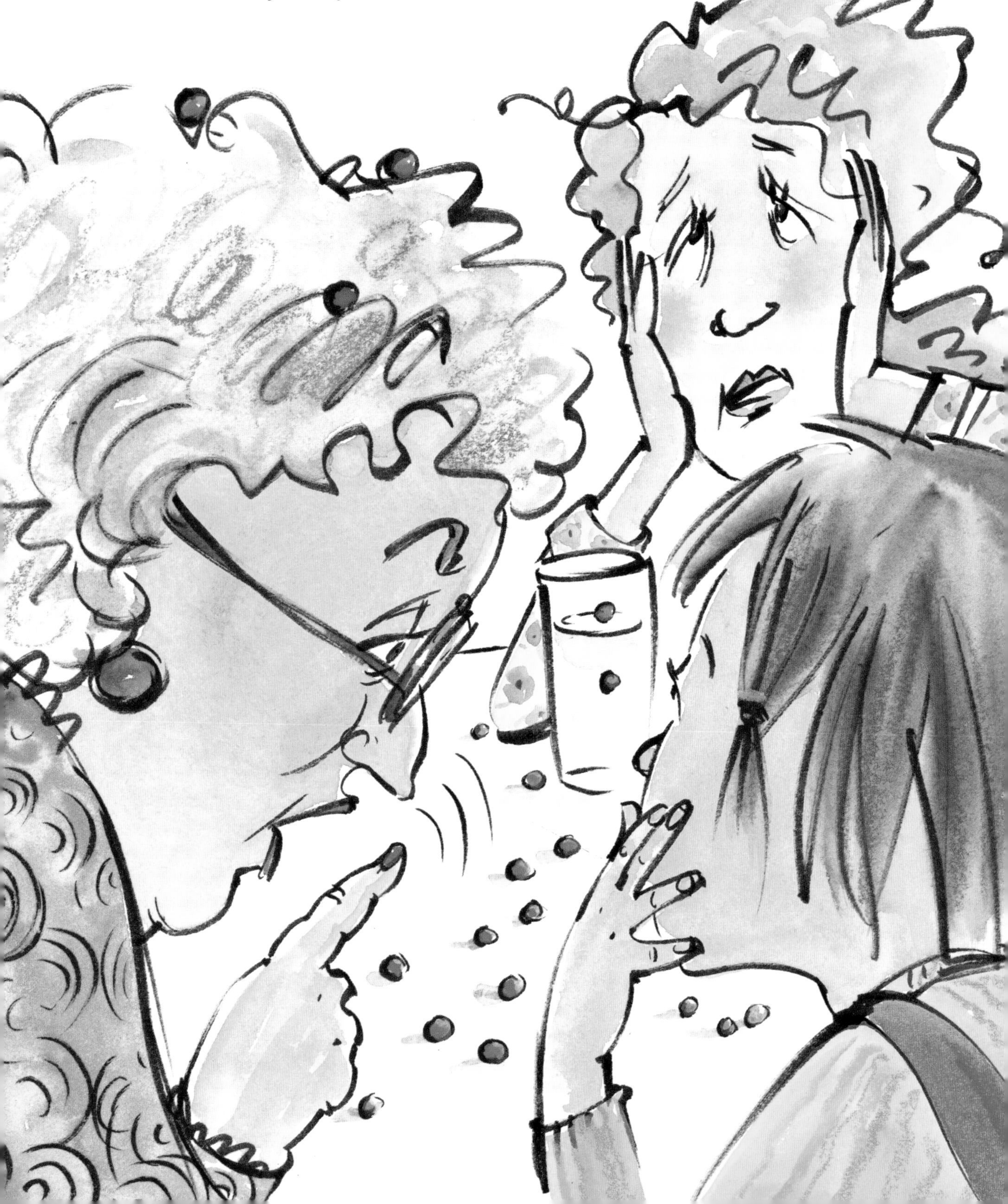

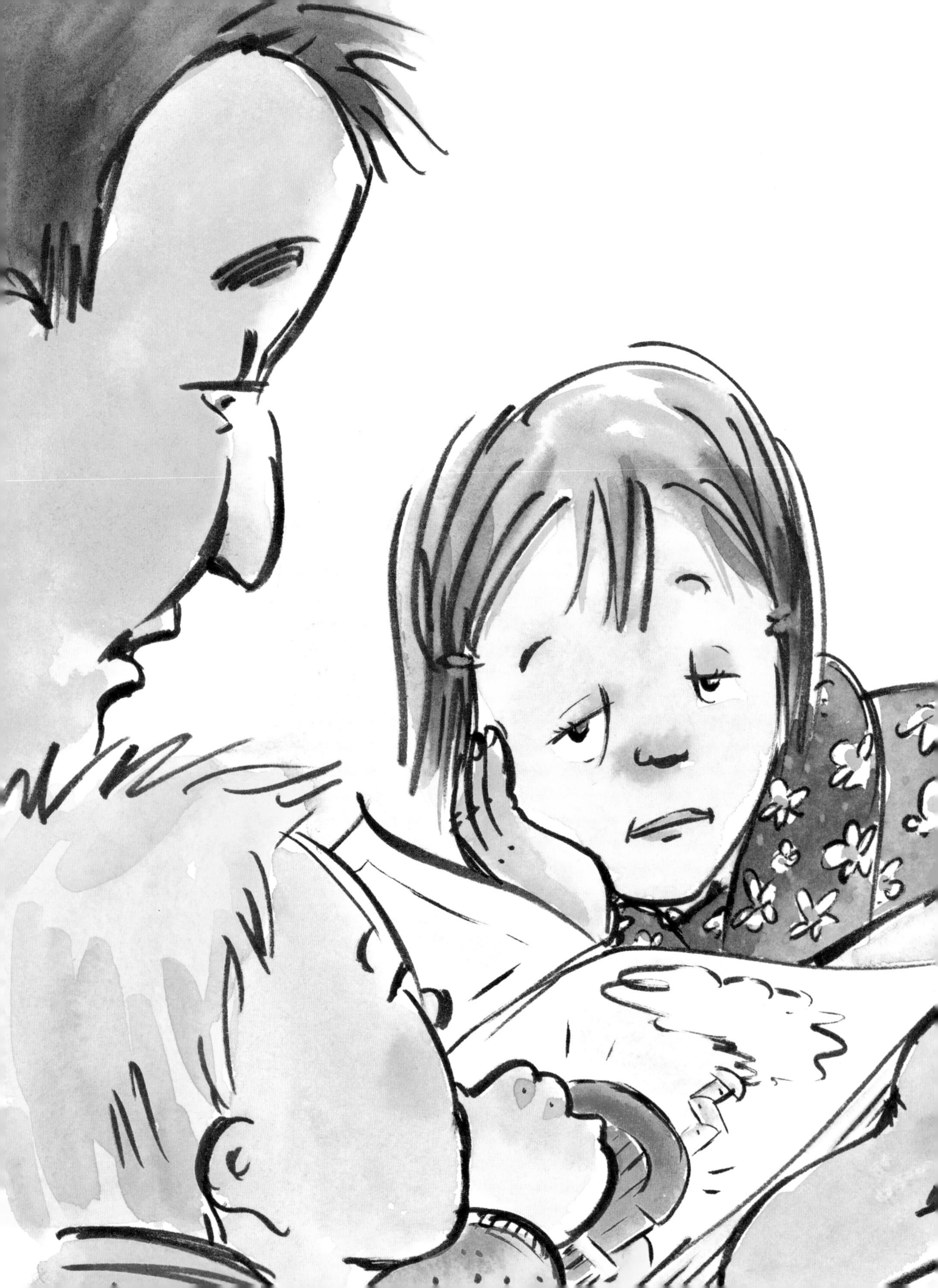

When it was time for a bedtime story, Louise knew, *she just knew*, that it wasn't going to be an easy ending to a not-so-easy day. Alex wanted Daddy to read *The Little Caboose,* but she wanted to hear *The Mystery of the Missing Cupcake.* To make things worse, Alex got the best spot on Daddy's lap, forcing Louise to squeeze, ever so unsteadily, onto the very corner of Daddy's knee.

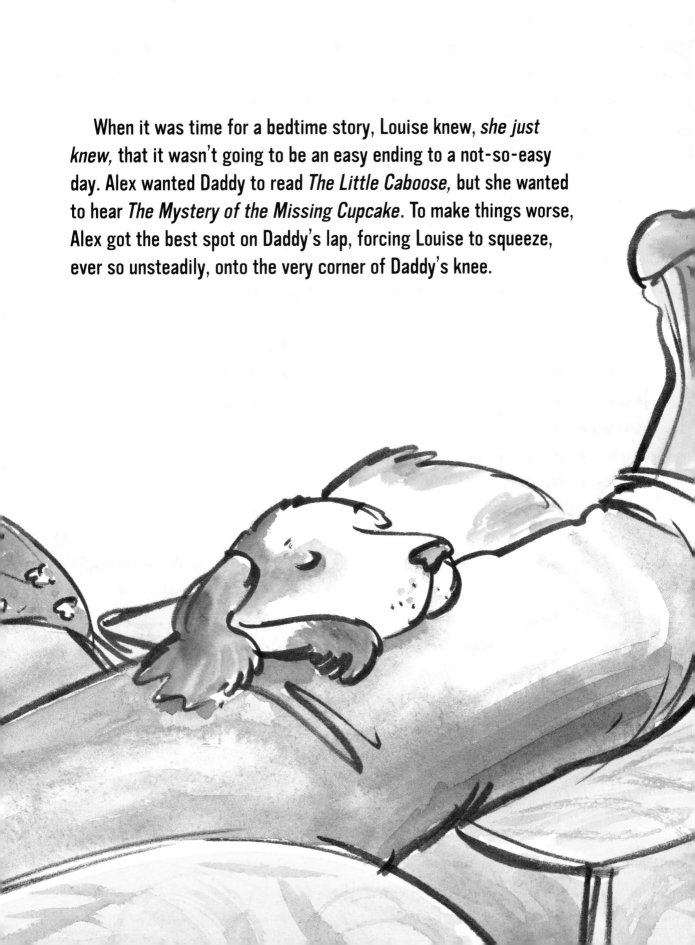

When Daddy started reading *The Little Caboose*, Louise's eyes got itchy, her throat got wheezy . . .

and her nose got sneezy. She knew that she was going to . . .

ACHOO!

Louise banged heads with Alex, who let out a piercing yell that startled Ginger the dog, who started to bark.

Louise lost her balance and tumbled off Daddy's knee.
"Geez, Louise! **COVER YOUR MOUTH, PLEASE!**" Daddy said
in an also-sort-of-barking voice.

That night, as Louise climbed into bed, she moaned to Bella Bear, "It's not easy when your eyes are itchy, your throat is wheezy, and your nose is very, very sneezy! I think I am allergic to oatmeal, spelling lists, pirouettes, peas, and, worst of all, my little brother!"

When Mommy and Daddy came into Louise's bedroom to tuck her in, Louise knew, *she just knew,* that they would not be in a very good mood.

But she was wrong.

"You didn't have a very easy day, did you?" Mommy asked in the softest Mommy voice ever.

"Seems you caught yourself a little cold," Daddy said in his warmest Daddy voice as he leaned over and kissed Louise on the head.

Just then, Louise's eyes got itchy, her throat got wheezy, and her nose got sneezy. She knew that she was going to . . .

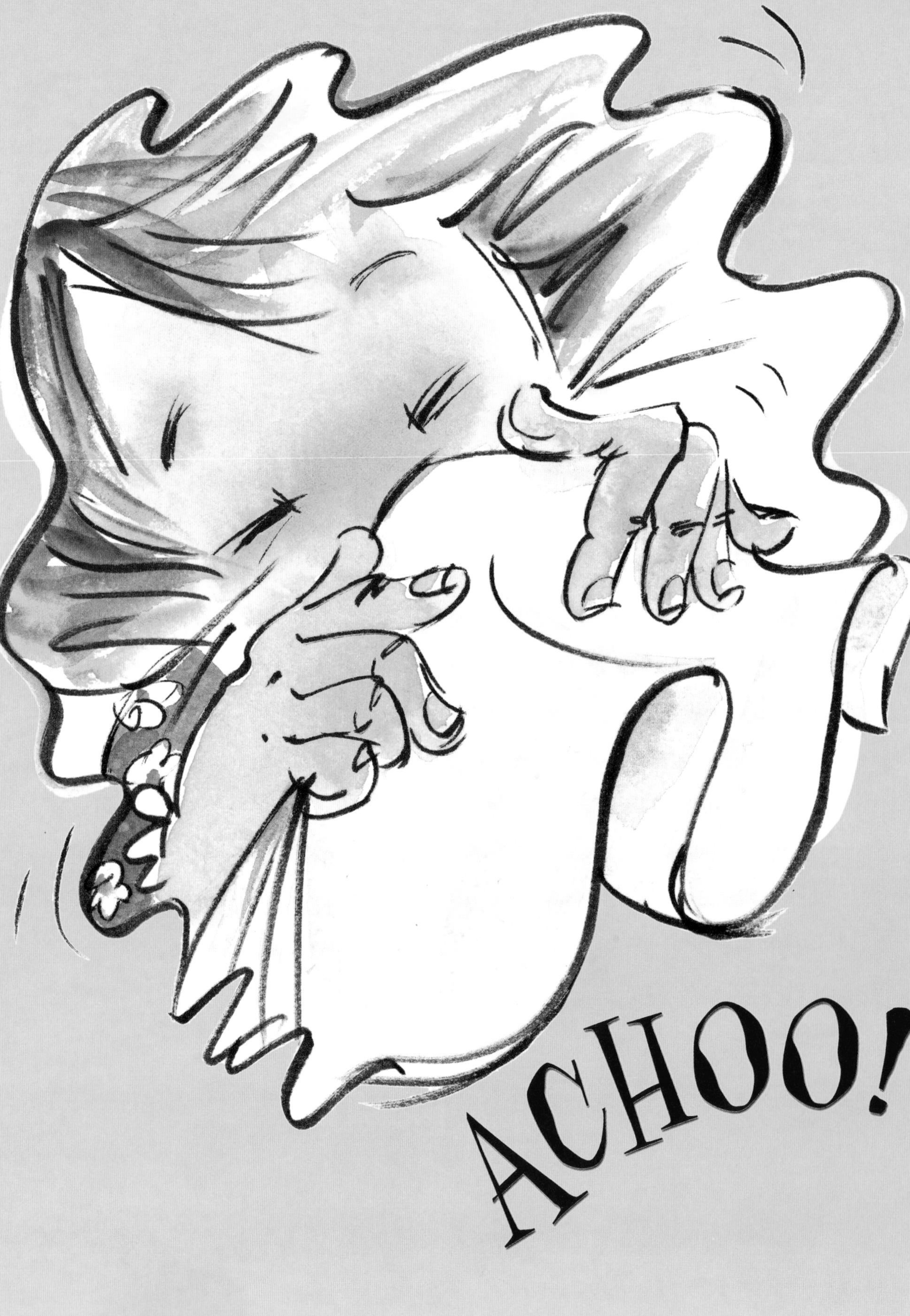
ACHOO!

Except this time, Louise was pleased that she remembered to cover her mouth when she sneezed!

"Gesundheit!" said Daddy, laughing.

Mommy and Daddy smiled her favorite Mommy and Daddy smiles. And Louise knew, *she just knew,* that tomorrow would be an easier day.

"Sweet dreams, sweet Louise!"

To Hannah Weis, Cameron Koehler,
and "special" children everywhere,
for their unconditional love and inspiration,
and
to their parents, for the compassion to "pay it forward."

And to Zach and Connor with all my love.
−I.B.

For Lottie.
−J.P.

Text copyright © 2009 by Irene Breznak
Illustrations copyright © 2009 by Janet Pedersen

All rights reserved.
Published in the United States by Random House Children's Books, a division of Random House, Inc., New York.

Random House and colophon are registered trademarks of Random House, Inc.

Visit us on the Web! www.randomhouse.com/kids

Educators and librarians, for a variety of teaching tools, visit us at www.randomhouse.com/teachers

Library of Congress Cataloging-in-Publication Data
Breznak, Irene.
Sneezy Louise / by Irene Breznak ; illustrated by Janet Pedersen. − 1st ed.
p. cm.
Summary: When Louise wakes up with itchy eyes, a wheezy throat, and a
sneezy nose, she just knows it is not going to be a very good day.
ISBN 978-0-375-85169-8 (trade) − ISBN 978-0-375-95169-5 (lib. bdg.)
[1. Sneezing−Fiction.] I. Pedersen, Janet, ill. II. Title.
PZ7.B7579Sn 2009
[E]−dc22
2007026720

MANUFACTURED IN CHINA
10 9 8 7 6 5 4 3 2 1

Random House Children's Book
 to read.

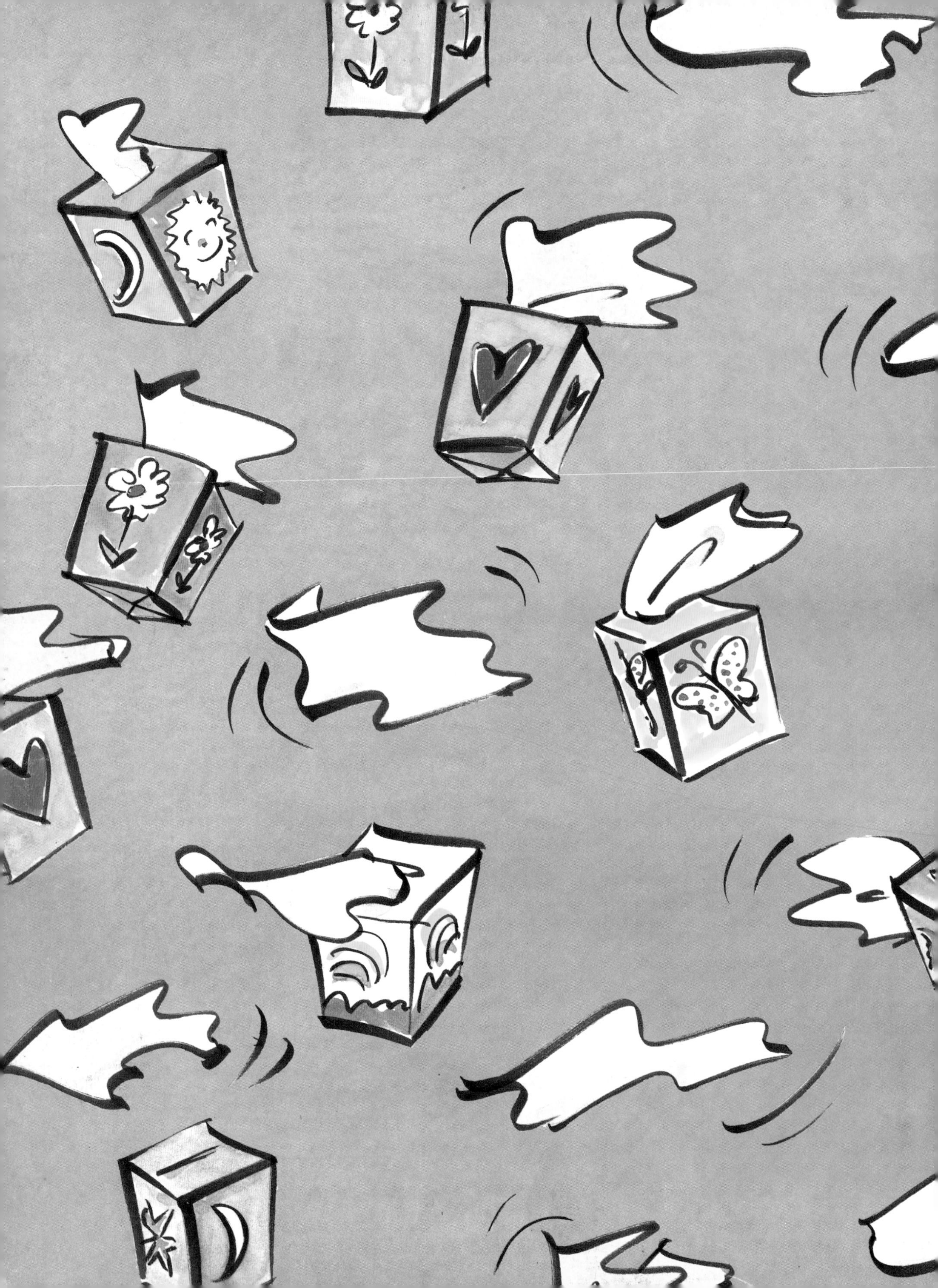